_____ *For* _____

Diana Mann, because.

IONA OPIE

_____ *For* _____

Amelia and Amy.

ROSEMARY WELLS

HERE COMES MOTHER GOOSE

edited by

IONA OPIE

illustrated by

ROSEMARY WELLS

WALKER BOOKS
AND SUBSIDIARIES
LONDON · BOSTON · SYDNEY

HERE COMES MOTHER GOOSE

Long ago, when the troubadours still roamed the lanes of Europe, a wise old bird called Mother Goose began to save small fragments of the songs that people most enjoyed. (She was called Frau Gosen in those days.)

As she wandered, she overheard men singing as they worked in the fields, and women singing as they rocked their babies to sleep, and she kept the songs warm under her wings. She listened to children at their play, and to grandads in chimney corners, reciting the sagacious distichs they had learned from *their* grandfathers. She invented rhymes to help babies find out where their eyes and noses are, and rhymes to help older children learn their numbers and the alphabet.

Nonsense verses she liked, and clever riddles. And more than all the others she liked the songs that run in people's heads and make them skip instead of walk, or dance around a room all on their own. This immortal lady has never stopped collecting; from every century she has stashed away the best.

IMPTY 1 DIMPTY 2 TIPSY-TEE 3 OKA-POKA 4 DOMINEE 5

When Mother Goose discovered how much *nicer* children are when fed on nursery rhymes, she published the rhymes in little books and added illustrations. The first, *Tommy Thumb's Pretty Song Book*, 1744, measured but 3 x 1¾ inches, and was adorned with thirty-six miniature engravings. Now, 250 years or so later, we have a book big enough to hide behind in a railway carriage, and as full of colour and revelry as anyone could long for on a grey winter's day. Rosemary Wells has created a host of memorable characters: cosy mother rabbits, cheeky ducklings, resolute and responsible dogs, adventurous cats. A family of guinea pigs act as clowns. They turn cartwheels and stand on their heads (an upside-down guinea pig is called a "pinny gig"). Ten of them, below, persuade us that topsy-turvy and frack-to-bont is the most delightful way to live: their names are

Impty, Dimpty, Tipsy-tee,

Oka-poka, Dominee;

Hocus-pocus, Dominocus,

Om, Pom, and Tosh.

Iona Opie

HOCUS-POCUS
6
DOMINOCUS
7
8
OM
POM
9
TOSH
10

Mabel, Mabel,
strong and able,

Take your elbows
off the table.

6

Contents

One-ery, two-ery, tickery, ten,
Bobs of vinegar, gentlemen.
A bird in the air,
a fish in the sea,
A bonny wee lassie
came singing to me.

Chapter One
1, 2, Buckle My Shoe

1 2
Buckle my shoe;

3 4
Knock at the door;

5 6

Pick up sticks;

7 8

Lay them straight;

9 10

A big fat hen.

Mary, Mary, quite contrary,
How does your garden grow?
With silver bells and cockleshells,
And pretty maids all in a row.

Hot cross buns, hot cross buns;
 One a penny poker,
Two a penny tongs,
Three a penny fire shovel,
Hot cross buns.

 had a sausage,
a bonny
bonny sausage,
I put it
in the oven
for my tea.

I went down
the cellar,
to get the
salt and pepper,
And the sausage
ran after me.

Bobby Shaftoe's gone to sea,
Silver buckles at his knee;
He'll come back and marry me,
Bonny Bobby Shaftoe.

17

ld King Cole

Was a merry old soul

And a merry old soul was he;

He called for his pipe

And he called for his bowl

And he called for his fiddlers three.

Cross-patch, draw the latch,
Sit by the fire and spin;
Take a cup, and drink it up,
Then call your neighbours in.

I had a little hen
The prettiest ever seen;
She washed up the dishes,
And kept the house clean.

She went to the mill
To fetch me some flour,
And always got home
In less than an hour.

Brush hair, brush,

The men are gone
to plough,
If you want to brush
your hair,
Brush your
hair now.

Jelly on a plate,
  Jelly on a plate,
Wibble, wobble, wibble, wobble,
Jelly on a plate.

Sausage in a pan,
Sausage in a pan,
Frizzle, frazzle, frizzle, frazzle,
Sausage in a pan.

Baby on the floor,
Baby on the floor,
Pick him up, pick him up,
Baby on the floor.

What are little girls made of, made of?

What are little girls made of?

Frogs and snails and puppy-dogs' tails,

That's what little girls are made of.

What are little boys made of, made of?

What are little boys made of?

Sugar and spice and all things nice,

That's what little boys are made of.

Simple Simon met a pieman,

Going to the fair;

Says Simple Simon to the pieman,

Let me taste your ware.

Says the pieman to Simple Simon,

Show me first your penny;

Says Simple Simon to the pieman,

Indeed, I have not any.

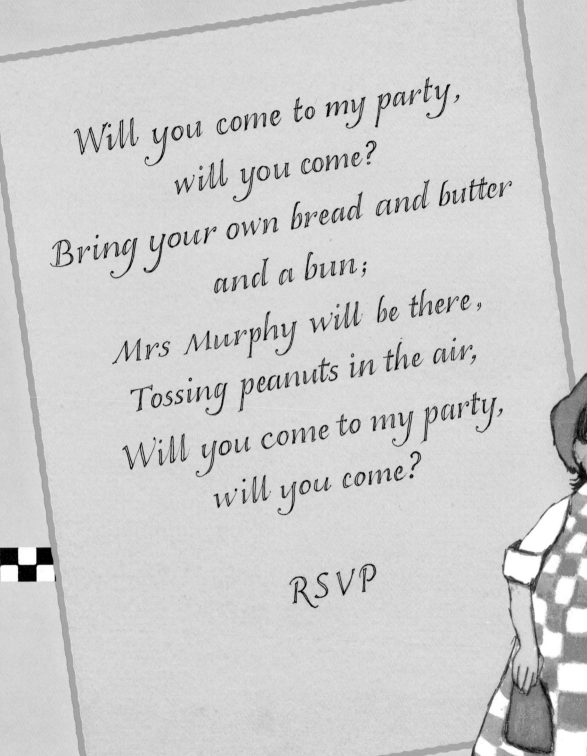

Will you come to my party,
will you come?
Bring your own bread and butter
and a bun;
Mrs Murphy will be there,
Tossing peanuts in the air,
Will you come to my party,
will you come?

RSVP

29

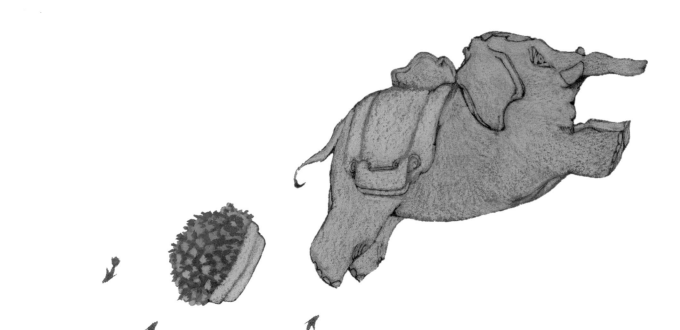

I asked my mother for fifty cents,

   To see the elephant jump the fence,

He jumped so high,

   He reached the sky,

And didn't come back till the Fourth of July.

Red sky at night,
Shepherd's delight;

Red sky in the morning,
Shepherd's warning.

Chapter Two
Old Mother Hubbard

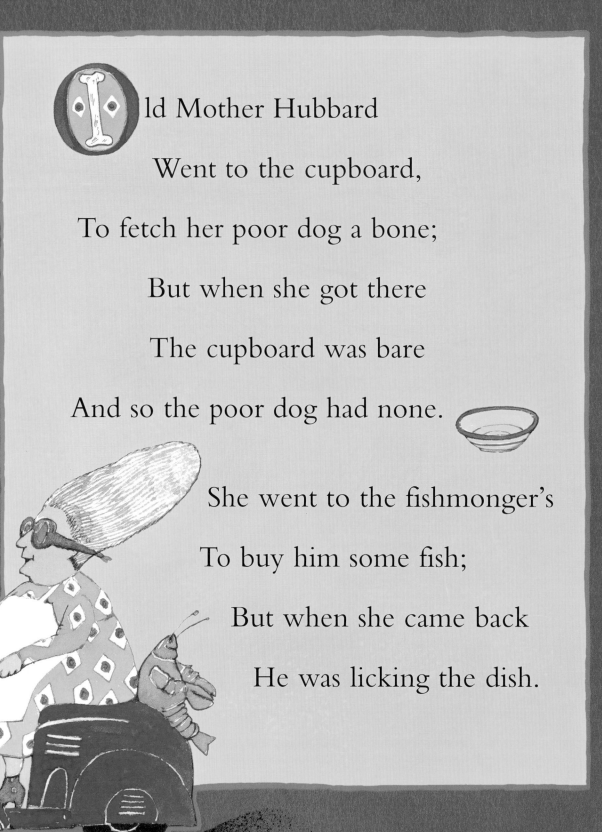

Old Mother Hubbard

Went to the cupboard,

To fetch her poor dog a bone;

But when she got there

The cupboard was bare

And so the poor dog had none.

She went to the fishmonger's

To buy him some fish;

But when she came back

He was licking the dish.

She went to the fruiterer's

To buy him some fruit;

But when she came back

He was playing the flute.

I'm Dusty Bill
From Vinegar Hill,
Never had a bath
And I never will.

Early in the morning at eight o'clock
You can hear the postman's knock;
Up jumps Ella to answer the door,
One letter, two letters, three letters, four!

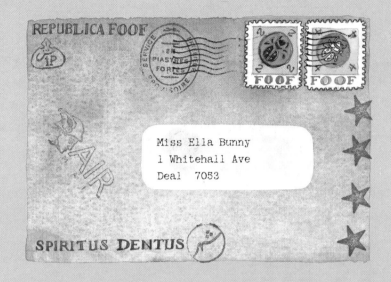

My Aunt Jane,

She came from France,

To teach to me the polka dance;

First the heel,

And then the toe,

That's the way

The dance should go.

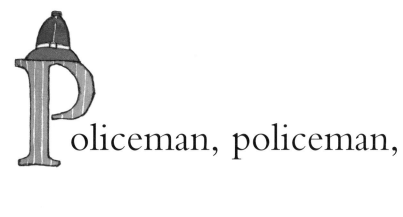

oliceman, policeman,

do your duty,

Here comes Freda the American beauty,

She can wiggle, she can waggle,

She can do the high kicks,

But I bet your bottom dollar

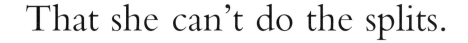

That she can't do the splits.

Here we go round

the mulberry bush,

The mulberry bush,

the mulberry bush;

Here we go round

the mulberry bush,

On a cold and frosty morning.

Little Tommy Tucker
Sings for his supper;
What shall we give him?
Brown bread and butter.
How shall he cut it
Without e'er a knife?
How will he be married
Without e'er a wife?

My mother and father are Irish,

We live upon Irish stew;

We bought a fiddle for ninepence,

And that was Irish too.

The wood was dark,
The grass was green,

My mother said
That I never should

I paid ten shillings
For an old blind horse;

Up comes Sally
With a tambourine;

Play with the pixies
In the wood;

I jumped on his back
And off in a crack,

I went to the river,
I couldn't get across,

Sally tell my mother
That I'm coming right back.

I saw a ship a-sailing,
A-sailing on the sea,
And oh, but it was laden
With pretty things for thee!

The captain was a duck
With a packet on his back,
And when the ship began to move
The captain said, Quack! Quack!

The cat's got the measles,
The measles, the measles,
The cat's got the measles,
Whatever shall we do?

We'll send for the doctor,
The doctor, the doctor,
We'll send for the doctor,
And he'll know what to do.

Manchester Guardian,

Evening News,

Here comes a cat

In high-heeled shoes.

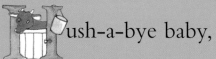ush-a-bye baby,

They're gone to milk,

Lady and milkmaid all in silk,

Lady goes softly, maid goes slow,

Round again,

round again,

round they go.

Chapter Three
As I Was Going to St Ives

A̶s̶ I was going to St Ives,   I met a man

with seven wives.　Each wife had seven sacks.

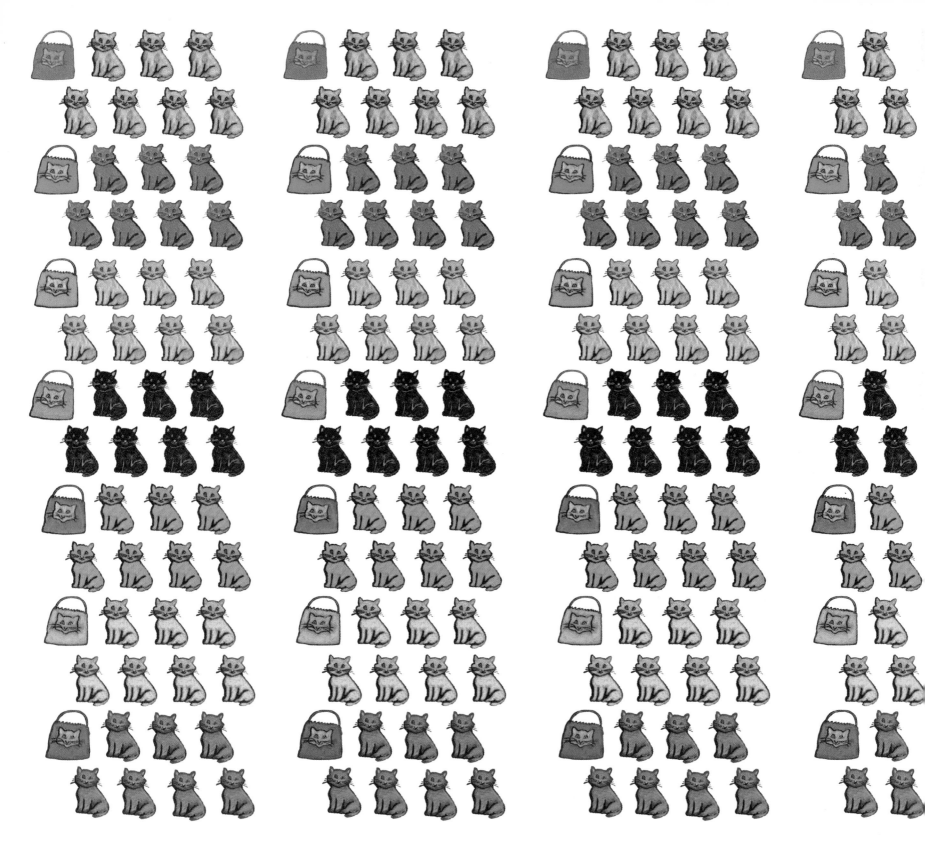

Each sack had seven cats.

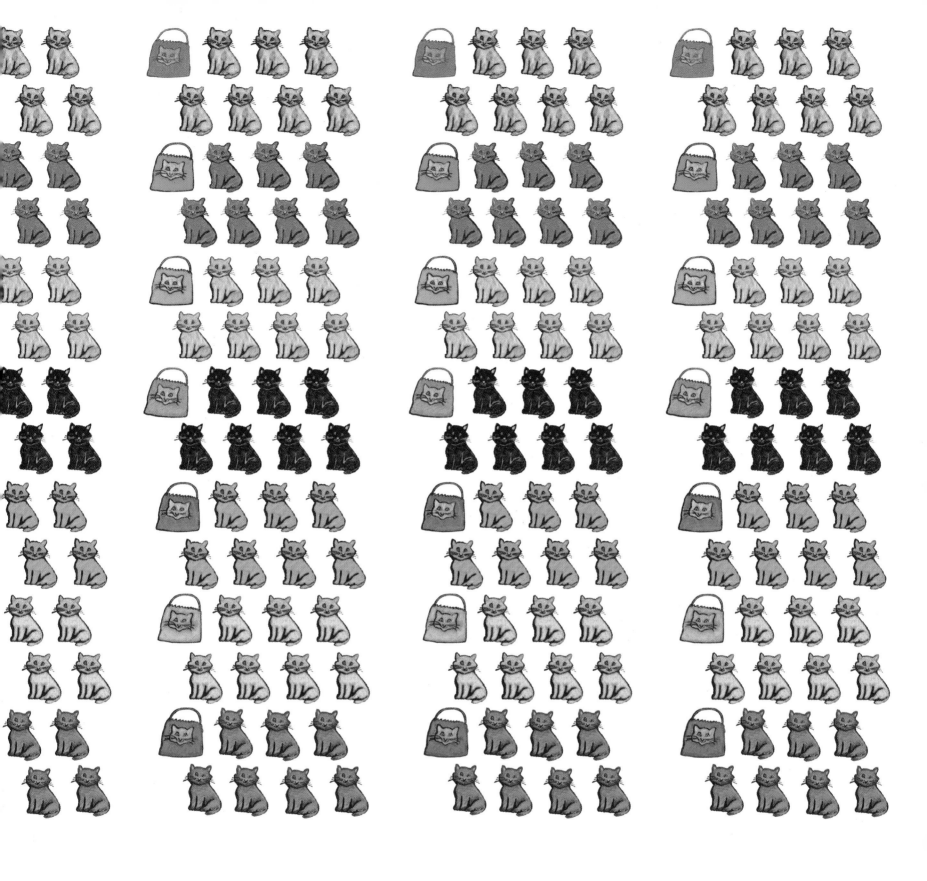

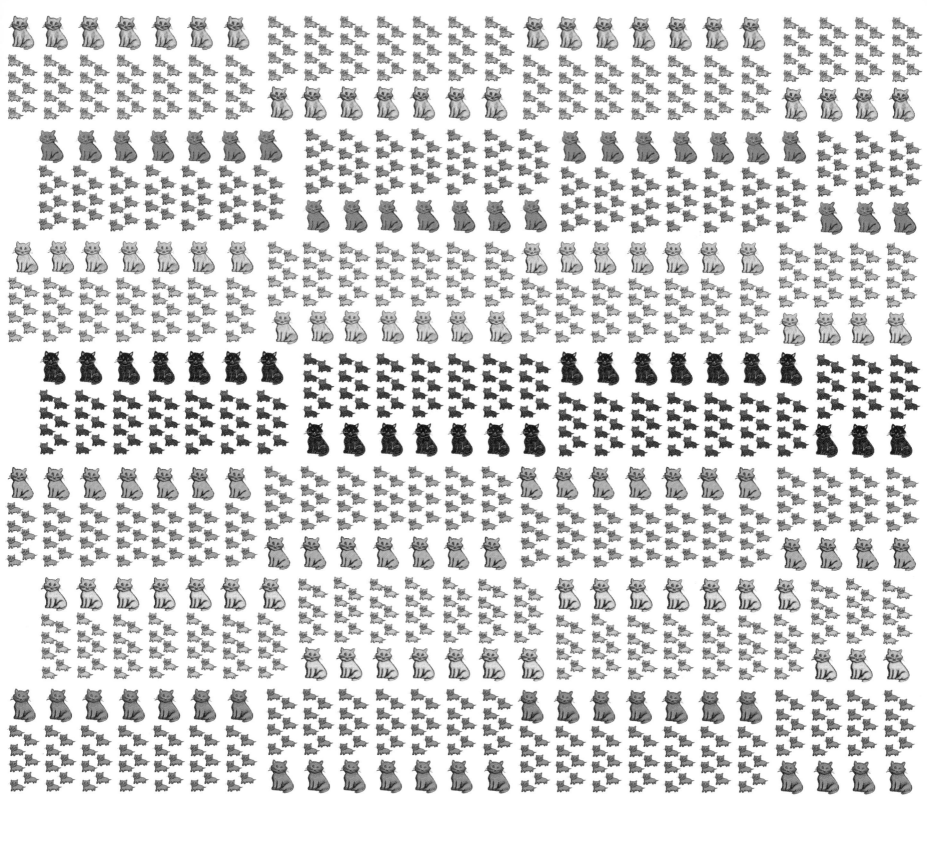

Each cat had seven kits.   Kits, cats, sacks and wives:

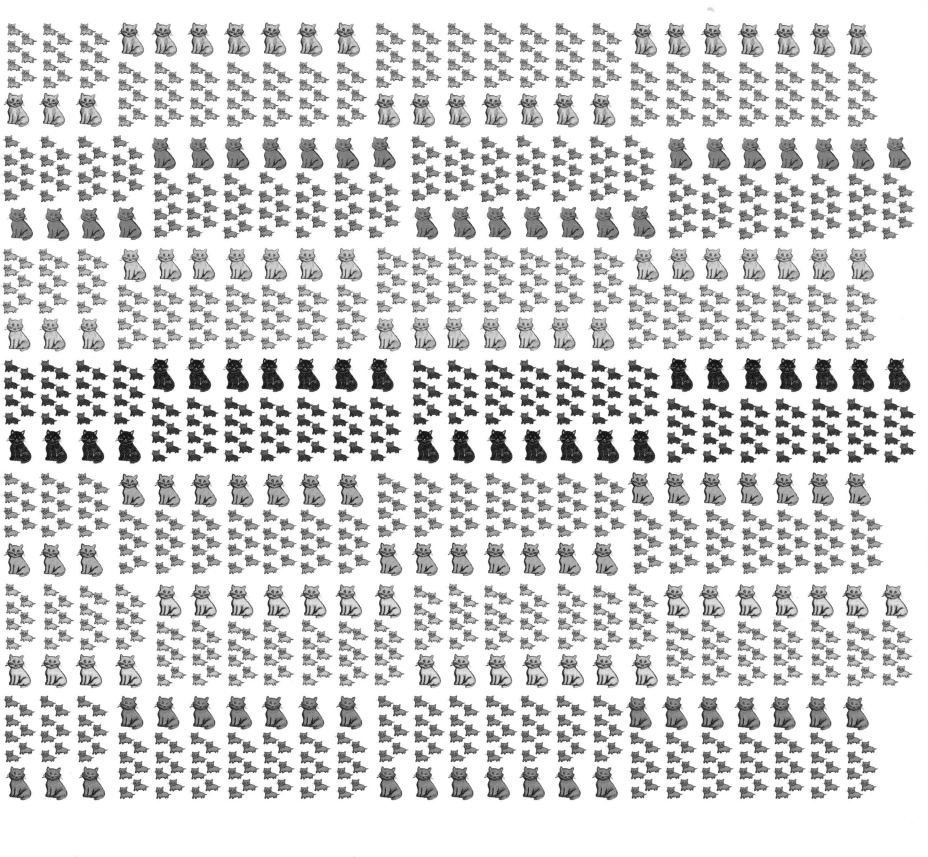

how many were there going to St Ives?

 had a little dolly dressed in green,

I didn't like the colour so

I sent it to the queen;

The queen didn't like it so

I sent it to the king,

The king said,

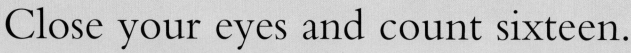

Close your eyes and count sixteen.

I am a Girl Guide
dressed in blue,

These are the actions

I must do:

Salute to the king,

Curtsey to the queen,

And turn my back to

the washing-machine.

bowline

square

clove hitch

Donkey, donkey, old and grey,

Open your mouth and gently bray.

Lift your ears and blow your horn

To wake the world this sleepy morn.

I'm a little teapot, short and stout,

Here's my handle,

Here's my spout.

When the tea is ready, hear me shout,

Pick me up and

Pour me out!

My ma's a millionaire,

Sky-blue eyes

and curly hair;

She can

play the violin,

Sitting on a biscuit tin.

Oranges and lemons,

Say the bells of St Clement's.

St Clement Danes

St Mary Whitechapel

Two sticks and an apple,

Say the bells at Whitechapel.

Kettles and pans,

Say the bells at St Anne's.

St Anne's Soho

St Martin-in-the-Fields

You owe me five farthings,

Say the bells of St Martin's.

When will you pay me?

Say the bells at Old Bailey.

St Sepulchre Old Bailey

St Leonard's Shoreditch

When I grow rich,

Say the bells at Shoreditch.

Pray when will that be?

Say the bells at Stepney.

St Dunstan Stepney

St Mary-le-Bow, Cheapside

I'm sure I don't know,

Says the great bell at Bow.

P ease porridge hot,

Pease porridge cold,

Pease porridge in the pot,

Nine days old.

le palmier

la cuillère

le chapeau

Christopher Columbus
was a very great man,
He sailed to America
in an old tin can.

The can was greasy,
And it wasn't very easy,
And the waves grew higher,

and higher,

and higher.

Wake up, baby, day's a-breaking,

Peas in the pot and a hoe-cake baking.

Diddle, diddle, dumpling,

my son John,

Went to bed with his trousers on;

One shoe off,

and one shoe on,

Diddle, diddle, dumpling,

my son John.

Twinkle, twinkle,

little star,

How I wonder what you are!

Up above the world so high,

Like a diamond in the sky.

Chapter Four
I Danced
with the
Girl

I danced with the girl

With a hole in her stocking,

And her heel kept a-rocking,

And her heel kept a-rocking;

I danced with the girl

With a hole in her stocking,

We danced by the light of the moon.

Bluebells, cockleshells,

Evie, ivie, over,

Mother's in the kitchen

Doing a bit of stitching,

Baby's in the cradle

Playing with a rattle,

A rickety stick, a walking stick,

One, two, three.

Mademoiselle she went to the well,
She didn't forget her
soap and towel;
She washed her hands,
she wiped them dry,
She said her prayers,
and jumped up high.

Tinker, tailor,

Soldier, sailor,

Rich man, poor man,

Ploughboy,

Thief.

Peter, Peter, pumpkin eater,

Had a wife and couldn't keep her;

He put her in a pumpkin shell

And there he kept her very well.

90

Sieve my lady's oatmeal, grind my lady's flour,

Put it in a chestnut, let it stand an hour.

My father's a king and my mother's a queen,

My two little sisters are dressed all in green.

Sukey, you shall
be my wife
And I will tell you why:
I have got a little pig,
And you have got a sty;

I have got a
dun cow,
And you can make good cheese;
Sukey, will you marry me?
Say Yes, if you please.

The Queen of Hearts
  She made some tarts,
    All on a summer's day;

94

The Knave of Hearts
He stole the tarts,
And took them clean away.

Down in the valley where the green grass grows,

There's a pretty maiden she grows like a rose;

She grows, she grows, she grows so sweet,

She sings for her true love across the street.

Tommy, Tommy, will you marry me?

Yes, love, yes, love, at half past three.

Ice cakes, spice cakes, all for tea,

We'll have our wedding at half past three.

Ride a cock horse

To Banbury Cross,

To see what Tommy can buy;

A penny white loaf,

A penny white cake,

And a two-penny apple pie.

As I was walking through the City,

Half past eight o'clock at night,

There I met a Spanish lady,

Washing out her clothes at night.

First she rubbed them, then she scrubbed them,

Then she hung them out to dry,

Then she laid her hands upon them

Said: I wish my clothes were dry.

 El Jabón   La Luna   La Camisa

Away down east,

away down west,

Away down Alabama,

The only girl that I love best

Her name is Susianna.

Come, crow! Go, crow!

   Baby's sleeping sound,

And the wild plums grow in the jungle,

   Only a penny a pound.

Only a penny a pound, Baba,

   Only a penny a pound.

There was a man of double deed
Sowed his garden full of seed.
When the seed began to grow,
'Twas like a garden full of snow.

INDEX OF FIRST LINES

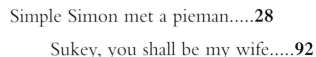

First published 1999 by Walker Books Ltd
87 Vauxhall Walk, London SE11 5HJ

2 4 6 8 10 9 7 5 3 1

This selection © 1999 Iona Opie
Illustrations © 1999 Rosemary Wells

This book has been typeset in M Bembo.

Printed in Italy

British Library Cataloguing in Publication Data
A catalogue record for this book is
available from the British Library.

ISBN 0-7445-5554-X